PAID IN OWN TOKEN

Paid In Own Token

Anelechi Bon Agoha

ISBN: 978-1-957724-02-7 (Paperback Edition)
ISBN: 978-1-957724-03-4 (Hardcover Edition)
ISBN: 978-1-957724-01-0 (E-book Edition)

Some characters and events in this book are fictitious. Any similarity to the real persons, living or dead, is coincidental and not intended by the author.

Book Ordering Information

Phone Number: 315 288-7939 ext. 1000 or 347-901-4920
Email: info@globalsummithouse.com
Global Summit House
www.globalsummithouse.com

Printed in the United States of America

Dedication

To my beloved late parents, Emily Nwankpa Agoha, nee Dappa and Bertram Merenini Agoha, aka, "Nnayi BM" for their selfless endeavors to my upbringing and education. Though, heart wrenching you are not here to witness my first literary milestone, you are always in my thought.

Table of Contents

Acknowledgement

My special admiration to my children, Pearl Nnenna, Britney Ozichi, and Princeton Chibuike Agoha who are the embodiments of my joy and happiness. Shout out to all my siblings, nieces and nephews for the good times and challenges we share. Humble appreciation to Chris Obi Nwakoby for his sponsorship on this project, and lastly, my gratitude to Bro Ken Oleru for his deserving "Big brother" role in my life.

Synopsis

The exodus of African men to Europe, U.S., and other developed parts of the world for greener pasture due to the continent's continuous economic recession seem to be a way out of epidemics of economic crunch menacing the continent.

By African culture and tradition, an average African male is family-oriented; hence, as they travel out, they never hesitated to either travel with their already formed nucleus families, or those not yet married to their former acquaintances coming back home to fulfill their commitment obligations to their loved ones. Although having good intentions of building a family with person of similar or same ethnicity and cultural background sounds plausible and intriguing, "Paid in Own Token," reveals otherwise. It typically unveils how dollar power pushes African sisters to marriage of cynicism and self-aggrandizement. It may be pertinent to state that the story of "Paid in Own Token" is set on the premise that, African-sisters outside African hemisphere in general and U.S.A.

in particular wreck brothers' marriage hopes and aspirations with their hidden marriage agenda fueled by dollar power for marriages that only work for them. However, there are exceptions to this notion, and I wish to express my sincere kudos to those exceptional.

You are hereby welcome to find out what transpired after Chyke gave it all to marry his home-based sweetheart, Amanda with his conventional marriage aspirations, but his hopes dashed against the walls. In addition, how unexpectedly, he finds comfort and joy with American woman, Keisha. While his estranged wife, Amanda got paid in own token in a relationship stunt with her like, Hector that started within church arena with dramatic and abrupt end on a street corner.

While part two of this literary work addresses some underlying issues with Africa and Africans as a people under the caption "Africa, Our Mother-Land"

PART 1

Chapter One

After about 14 flight hours and 6 transit hours, totaling about 20 hours trip from Nigeria, Amanda could not wait for her arrival to Dulles International Airport, Dulles, Virginia in Washington, DC Metro Area of the United States of America to meet her husband, Chyke after their last meeting of about 16 months ago in Nigeria. While Chyke full of gladness and excitement was delighted to have a wife added to his early accomplishments as he raced to the airport to have his wife, Amanda picked up.

Amanda waited just briefly for Chyke's arrival after being cleared from arrival/immigrations protocols. Their meeting full of pleasantries that was dominated with lots of unending hugs as Chyke loads her middle-sized Samsung luggage into his car trunk. Prior to Chyke's driving out, Amanda requested for use of ladies room as she stated she is been long pressed but was only anxious to the sight of her man, Chyke first.

Headed to his apartment building located at Twin Towers Apartment in Bladensburg, Maryland; Chyke took to Interstate 395 North as to use the opportunity to initiate City site seeing of part of Arlington, Virginia, crossing through 14th Street bridge to Washington, DC to his love, Amanda reroutes to his destination of Bladensburg, Maryland. Both were full of excitements, joy, and smiles, as they romantically touched and tickled each other as Chyke bombards Amanda with questions of their parents' and other relatives' welfare till they got off building elevator that took them to the 10th floor to Chyke's apartment.

Amanda refreshes herself with warm water shower, and now is eating on the dining table with Chyke, as they both look at each other in intense happiness in discussing her trip and Amanda extending her parent's pleasantries and gratitude to her husband, Chyke. And at the same time expressing his gratitude to God for journey mercy and how it all worked out well for her to make it here starting from her visa interview without hitches. You can never ask for any better than this, he said.

Amanda has been so pleasant and loving to Chyke as both started feeling the joy of married life and that being together seemed to be the best thing that both had craved for since the beginning of their love life dating back to about three years before their formal marriage. They will intermittently tease each other about their love letters and late-night outings in some cases were against Amanda's protective parents' wishes.

After about five weeks of Amanda's arrival to the U.S. with zeal to get started for Dollar search, she has been home eating; drinking all sorts of juices loaded in the refrigerator and may be watching American strange TV shows she is yet to comprehend. On this fateful day, when her husband, Chyke came home from work, Amanda politely engaged him in an eagerness conversation:

Amanda – Chy, it seems I am beginning to rather feel bored seating here at home, without something to do while you are out to work; when are you going to get me a job?

Chyke –Perplexed as he busted into laughter – Ha! Ha!! Ha!!! Ha!!!! Sweetie, he calls her. There is a lay down process for that, and we already started that by submitting applications for both your Social Security Card and work permit/green card. They take a while to be out.

Amanda – So, one cannot work without those cards you mentioned?

Chyke – No ooh! You cannot legally do anything without them. Truly speaking, while waiting for your stuff to be out, I am contemplating on having you get started with acquiring some credit hours at one of these colleges at after the arrival of your Social Security, preferably PG

Community College. The work thing may come later.

Amanda – Kind of jumped up from her seating position – why? Why can't I start working to make some money as to help both here and people at home? You know our peoples' expectations. They will soon be expecting something from me.

Chyke – Who are those? Expecting what from someone who just got here? Listen my dear; life is generally more complex than expected when not properly planned with solid foundation like education. Excuse me to use the old saying, thus: "You plan to fail when you fail to plan". You may recall my discussions with you on this subject matter when in Nigeria – This system is set up for one to almost (BA) begin again despite your previous education in most professional areas, talk less of one who hasn't even acquired one. I hope you see this as a golden opportunity for a second chance to better yourself as against meeting other peoples' expectations.

Amanda – Okay. But you still have some more explanations to do on why making some money is not better than whatever you're trying to come up with.

Chyke – Chill out sweetheart. Never mind, we still have plenty of time to work out what is best for us on a long term.

After couple of weeks, Chyke was able to put some money together for a shopping spree in which he showers his wife, Amanda with some love gifts with their visit to a shopping center. While Amanda returns her husband's favors as she hurriedly prepares him a special dish to eat upon their return to their apartment from shopping and after which she lures him to the bedroom for some very private moments.

In addition, in about three years fast gone into this amicable young couple's life, Amanda proceeds in her quest to finding her feet to the right direction in taking pre-requisite nursing classes. As may be expected, she has found herself a female socializing friend by name, Betsy. Life has been so cozy and pleasant for the couple as they strive to figure each other out. Not to mention that they have been blessed with a female child, Cindy for their first-born.

Chapter Two

In about five years into Chyke and Amanda's marriage in the United States, Amanda is now on her final semester to a Nursing program (RN), with a female child, Cindy to show for a fruitful marriage. She is now full of accomplished attitude, without respect to mankind.

On this blissful day as Amanda pays Betsy a visit to her residence. Hanging out at Betsy's living room with their girls talk:

Betsy – Amanda, you kind of look lost from time to time as I speak to you. What is it that is bordering you?

Amanda – When did you become a psychic? I am really losing it with my diminishing love for this guy I live with.

Betsy – Really, do you mean, Chyke your husband?

Amanda – Yea.

Betsy - That's a very big issue right there. I hope he doesn't have any idea of it?

Amanda – No. He doesn't. But, what do I do about this?

Betsy – I wish am a social counselor, my dear. Anyway, what do I get for you to drink? I've not even told you that I prepared some good vegetable soup. Would you like to have some?

Amanda – I don't have appetite for any food now. But, I would like to take some for carryout if you don't mind? For the drink, I'll fix myself some; May you please stop treating me like a quest in this place whenever am here? For am not one, please. Amanda sluggishly stood up from the couch and headed towards the refrigerator in the kitchen for a drink.

Here, Amanda was on international phone call conversation with her parents in her first time reveal to them of her impending clandestine plan of splitting from her husband, Chyke. With their conversation progressing, thus:

Amanda – ... I can now take care of myself and you guys without the help of any son of a man or whatever he calls himself; Yeah Mom, let me talk to Dad. Daddy, I was telling mom that I would be graduating at the end of this semester as a Registered Nurse. You know what that means? Huh! Money, I mean Dollar unlimited...

As Amanda continues her unbelievable phone conversation with her parents, yes, I have finally arrived. Please pray for me.

Chyke opens the front door and walks in as Amanda abruptly ended her phone call.

Chyke – Wow! What was that for?

Amanda – You don't need it. That was some family talk.

Chyke – With who, If you don't mind?

Amanda – Why all these interrogations?

Chyke – You called for it. I wonder why my wife will abruptly end a phone conversation as her husband walks into the house. Is someone hiding something here for no reason?

Amanda – You may call it whatever you choose.

Chyke – I warned you the other day about sewing seed of distrust with such behaviors.

Amanda – What happens if I do? Whatever!!!

Chyke turns back while walking into the bedroom and profusely looks at Amanda.

Amanda continues her to-be achiever attitude in a following conversation she had with Chyke, her husband:

Amanda - Chyke, what do you think about this place we still live at?

Chyke – What about it? I mean, what do you mean, "what do I think about this place we live at?"

Amanda – I thought you're the one who is always talking about reading one's spouse's mind? Why can you read my mind now to understand what I mean?

Chyke – Common now! Not this way. I wish you gave me a better lead to help me read this mind of yours.

Amanda – Okay. As I graduate in few weeks, Will it be out of place if I say we should be thinking, if not looking to move to a single-family home?

Chyke – Sarcastically, what a wonderful thought! Have you forgotten it's not quit too long we moved from Prince Georges County to here in Montgomery and now you coming up with another move idea? Why must we always be on the move as if that's all to be done to be successful in life? Anyway, that has never crossed my mind and has no need to at this time.

Amanda – What do you mean "that never crossed your mind?"

Chyke – Just as it sounds. That's not on my present list of worries, my dear.

Amanda – Why is it not? And when will it be on your so-called list of worries?

Chyke – When the time is right, we can talk about it, Sweetheart.

Amanda – That makes no sense to me. You've always talked about growth. Not anymore, right? May be the idea is from me and that makes it sound too strange and out of place? But you have to understand that when your time is right may not be when my time is right, okay?

Chyke – There we go again. You've always misquoted me with bias. This is not about the person presenting the issue. It's about prioritizing issues; I may have to say that the right perspective to this is that one should only bring up this issue if: The neighborhood has become bad; There is change in family size; or lastly, both of us are done with our studies and started making the expected differences in paychecks. But none of those prevails now. So, what's the rush? My philosophy has always been to spend on established affordability, rather than presumes affordability as to avert any sort of financial embarrassment.

Amanda – You're preaching to the choir. Again, when your time is right, may not be right for me, anyway.

Chyke – I presume you are not overwhelmed with this so-called "Nurses status quo" syndrome?

Despite their last conversation, coupled with her clandestine plans, Amanda engaged her friend, Betsy to help her locate a real estate agent, Anita who they visited her real estate's office in her quest for a new house without her husband's consent-

As they were welcomed into the office by Anita, Amanda was handed over some retainer paperwork to fill out prior to their engaging in her needs to real estate requirements.

Anita – Will you be the sole owner of this property you're about buying?

Amanda – Yes.

Anita – If you don't mind, I understand you're married.

Amanda – Yes, but not to be in not too long.

Betsy – Murmured, Oh my God!!

Anita – What's that?

Amanda – Please don't even mind her. That reminds me; is it true that the law stipulates that any property acquired in marriage by any of the parties automatically belong to both parties by common law marriage of this state?

Anita – Yes. It looks like you've already done your homework on this. That's a good thing as it is said that "The best customer is a well-informed customer" That means you really know what you're in for, right?

Amanda – May be!

Anita – Continues: Are you ready to start looking?

Amanda – Almost, l am looking at couple of job offers as I graduate in a few. So, I will like you to provide me with the requirements that I'll be working on when I start my new career.

Anita Provides some writing materials for Amanda to take note with as she calls out the requirements to her …

In addition, as soon as they stepped out of Anita's office, Betsy could not hold to engage Amanda in an open confrontational conversation, thus:

Betsy – Amanda, what would you really do about the common marriage law question you brought up? Will that not hamper your plan of sole ownership of the house?

Amanda – That's not a problem at all depending on your perspective to it. I will do whatever it takes to get rid of him before that time.

Betsy – Are you truly serious about all these craziness? You know, despite the odd of a single lady counseling on marriage affairs, my perspective is that of endurance to make room for progress if you ask me, as there might be nothing better out there. Besides, record indicates best things of life are better achieved working together.

Amanda – Better, believe it. That's the only option Am left with to beat the so-called common law of marriage.

Betsy – What can I say? I guess you're so determined.

Chapter Three

At the thought of this couple haven gone above and beyond marriage threshold of new couples, Amanda continues to unleash her surprised "End it all agenda" in pursuit of selfishness as she relentlessly invokes nastiness and contentiousness into her marriage with Chyke, as she continues her split plan from Chyke thus.

On this day, with Amanda complacently seating on the couch in the living room with legs on the center table, while on the phone as Chyke walks into the house. Chyke was in the house to grab a bit of homemade food before heading out to class at the University of Maryland where he is taking classes:

Chyke – Hey dear, what do you have in your kitchen? Please make me a quick fix before I head out. You know today is one of those my in and out days?

Amanda neither responded, nor made any move to attend to Chyke's request.

Chyke – Amanda, has it gotten to this? You ignored both my entrance into the house and now my request for something to eat before heading out to lectures?

Amanda *Snapped*; Chyke may I advise you to please get yourself in the kitchen to prepare yourself a meal if you're hungry and must eat. I don't have that time for you now. Yea, you think you're in a restaurant. Amanda this, Amanda that. I'm not your house girl, okay? This is America, please.

Chyke – Did I hear you right? "This is America, huh?"

Amanda – You heard me right.

Chyke – I can now read the handwriting on the wall. You're senselessly getting out of control, and I will live to see where these leads.

Amanda – Snapped again and jumped Chyke; who is getting out of senseless what?

– Chyke tries to avoid Amanda's physical confrontation. But, to no avail. Amanda continues her offensive assaults, while Chyke minimally defends back till he had a chance to subdue her when she ran out of gas. But, when let go by Chyke, Amanda makes a quick move to the phone and dilled 911. Panting and crying…

Amanda – "he will kill me if no one gets here quickly"

Police Dispatcher – Who will kill you?

Amanda – Chyke, my husband. He jumped me

Police Dispatcher – Ma-am, Ma-am; someone will be there shortly. Please stay on the line with me. Did you say your husband?

Amanda – Yea, yes.

Police Dispatcher – Does he have a weapon? I mean, can you see any gun on him?

Amanda – No. eem! I don't know.

Police siren is heard on the background. Shortly, there was a bang on the entrance door as the police announces; Montgomery County Police, open the door.

Chyke unlocks the entrance door, and the police officer walks into the house as Amanda continues with her fake cry for help.

Police Officer – I am Officer Bill of Montgomery County Police Department. Someone called in for domestic violence here. Pointing at Amanda, you called 911?

Amanda - Acknowledges with a node.

Police Officer – Pointing towards Chyke, what's your name?

Chyke – Am Chyke

Police Officer – Directing his question to Amanda; what happened?

Amanda – Faking to cry, she responds, He is an ingrate, for all I have done serving him. Just for not making his food ready on time for the first time like a slave will do for her master, he got furious, yelling at me; slapping and beating me up. I can't take this anymore. She continues her fake cry.

Police Officer – directing his question to Chyke, was that true?

Chyke – None of those is true at all. Just believe me. Am saying the truth…

Police Officer – Neither believing, nor giving Chyke the opportunity to defend himself, he orders; please step aside.

Chyke – Moves to the direction of his orders but continues to murmur – I can't believe this happening. I cannot believe you can lie on me in a heartbeat just like that, furiously looking at Amanda.

Police Officer – Hey! I don't want you to say anything to her anymore. Do you understand that?

Chyke – Yes. But this is unbelievable.

Police Officer – While I'm still here, seeing the tension of the situation, I want you to go in to get some of your personal effects and go out temporarily to somewhere. May be sleep out to a friend or family member's house to allow temper to cool-off. This is a domestic dispute that I do not have the authority to rule on. If she feels uncomfortable with you being around, she may have to file for protective order with a Judge in the district court. But, as I said, that's her decision to make.

After about 2 days past their last ordeal, as Chyke was in his study room for studies.

County Sheriff – Knocks on the door, and announces – Montgomery County Sheriff, please open the door.

Chyke answers the entrance door to let him in.

County Sheriff – I am Officer Daniels; Are you Mr. Chyke …?

Chyke – Yes, I am.

County Sheriff – Am here to serve you with an ex-parte order issued by a Judge of the Montgomery County District Court as filed against you by Mrs. Amanda Eze. I believe she leaves here too. I wish to explain this protective order to you. You are to vacate this residence immediately till you appear before the Judge in court at the stated date of hearing of the case as stated in this order. You cannot contact Mrs. Amanda Eze in person or by phone at home or her workplace. You cannot be seen within 50 yards of this residence or her workplace. And violation of any of these conditions will mean violation of Court order that will result to your immediate arrest and detention. So, you have about 10mins to pick up any personal items you may require before leaving out, per the order.

Chyke heads to the bedroom, escorted by the police officer to collect some of his personal effects and leaves to an unknown location in keeping with the ex-parte order.

Chapter Four

Betsy and her friend, Keisha hangs out in her apartment-home for some lady's gossip:

Betsy – Hey girlfriend, please come right in.

Keisha – I am so sorry that I just showed up at your door. I happen to be in the neighborhood, saw your car in the parking lot, and took a chance of meeting you at home. But, only found out that my cell died out as I tried calling you.

Betsy – Common on in. Never mind, girlfriend, that's not a problem. I have been home and bored to death all day. Just make yourself at home if you are not just here to recharge your cell.

Keisha – Not at all, girl. I don't even have my wall charger with me.

Betsy – Relax Keisha. That was a joke. But if you had it that could have been a plus while you're here. Unfortunately, I can't be of help in that department as we do not have same carrier or even same phone as they now make it extremely difficult, if not impossible for people to share phone accessories.

Keisha – Yea. It is all about "The Benjamin" Profit-maximization. They don't look out for us, but themselves.

Betsy – What can I get you to drink, please?

Keisha - Red wine, otherwise, OJ (orange juice)

Betsy – I hope you don't mind OJ; this economic crunch has slowed down my shopping habit, you may not believe what I don't have in this house that I need to get my black behind out to get as soon as conditions improve.

Keisha – Girl, you're full of it.

Betsy – What can I say? You know anything that goes wrong now you blame it on economic recession. Employers even use it best on employment frizz.

Keisha – Tell me about it. Even in the health profession.

Betsy – Forget those mean-spirited individuals, at a time nemesis will catch up with them. How was your day, girl friend? Betsy heads to her kitchen for Keisha's OJ

Keisha – Wonderful, just wonderful. God is good.

Betsy – Seats a glass full of OJ on the center table for Keisha and seats on the couch next to her. You know Keisha, I am happy you stopped by; you know my friend Amanda, right?

Keisha – Yea! What about her?

Betsy – Nothing really. But I must confess that I don't in any way understand what she is up to with her husband.

Keisha – What she is up to in what?

Betsy – My dear, all I get from her is that she is heading towards getting rid of her husband.

Keisha – Oh my God! You must report that to the authorities, if, you're sure.

Betsy – God. Please come down Keisha, not in that manner. Maybe I worded it wrongly. I meant to say she is, eem, she may be trying to call it quits with her husband, Chyke. And the poor guy doesn't even have a clue.

Keisha – Now you're talking. But divorce is no more a surprising issue in our time in this country. Although amongst you Africans it's a different ball game due to your cultural and traditional ties and even religious commitments, as I understand.

Betsy – Not just that. But how would she turn around to bite the finger that fed her? I mean all the while; she is not able to mention one bad habit of this guy that could be responsible for the path she is about to take.

Keisha – Are you saying as a friend, you don't agree with her reasons?

Betsy – Reasons? What reasons? She is just flat; didn't you hear me say she is unable to give one, not even one reason? All she says is that she continues to get less attracted to him.

Keisha – Yea, I know what you mean, there must be some sort of behavioral pattern from the man to justify such a drastic move, unless it's psychologically unknown.

Betsy – I strongly believe the unknown whatever may have a strong root from back home.

Keisha – What back home, from Africa? Do you mean voodoo as seen in some of those African movies?

Betsy – No Keisha; those are things of the past. The movies recreate them to show darkness of the past. But I mean family pressure; it may be financial independence crossing her mind now that she is about to start earning RN paycheck.

Keisha – That will be so silly of her. But hey, that puts the guy back in the market, right?

Betsy – What can I say, girlfriend?

Keisha – She must get it that guys are rear to come by; when dumped, someone else get to pick them up; It might as well be me, ok? Anyways, am here to ask of that your friend who comes with those designer bags for sale. When is she coming around? Are they boot legs or authentic?

Betsy – Oh Jessica! She travelled but will be back soon. Will let you know when she is back. I trust you can figure out them out yourself.

Court Orderly – All stand, Judge Jones presiding. All seat, please.

Judge Jones – Mrs. Eze vs. Mr. Eze; this is a case of domestic dispute.

Chyke and Amada came out from their various seats to take their defendant's and complainant's stands, respectively.

Judge Jones – Directing to Amanda: Plaintiff; please say your full names.

Amanda – My name is Amanda Eze

Judge Jones – Directing to Chyke: Defendant; please say your full names.

Chyke – My name is Chyke Eze

Judge Jones – Making general statement: I believe there was no violation of the ex-parte order as none was brought to my attention.

– Directing his question to Amanda: what happened on …?

Amanda - Eem! Eem! Eem! I don't know what I did wrong in getting married to him; nothing pleases him. He unnecessarily picks on me each time he's home; eem…

Judge Jones – Mrs. Eze, did you understand my question? I asked you to tell the court what happened between you and Mr. Chyke Eze on … that brought you here?

Amanda – I am sick and tired of being with him. I don't want him to ruin my life. I don't even need him to survive here anymore.

Judge Jones – Just stop right there. I don't intend repeating myself any further. I want you to explain what transpired between you and Mr. Eze that resulted to the 911 call of … and your subsequent filing of protective order against him. Do I make myself clear in this simple and plain language?

Amanda – Yes. But I had said I no longer want to be with him. I want a divorce.

Judge Jones – Snapped. We're not making any progress with this attitude of yours. Please sit down. Amanda retraces her steps to seat down on the chair/bench.

Judge Jones – Mr. Chyke Eze, could you please take the stand and tell the court what happened between you and Mrs. Amanda Eze on … that brought you before this court today?

Chyke – Thanks my lord. Technically, I don't know what I'm accused of. But, on that fateful day I came back home from work to have a quick eat of any available food in the house before going to my evening lectures at the University of Maryland; on getting home to my wife, Amanda (Chyke slightly pointed towards Amanda's direction). I respectfully and romantically requested my wife Amanda "Hey dear, what do you have in your kitchen? Please make me a quick fix before I head out. You know I have lectures today". She totally ignored my request, despite even ignoring my entry into the house, which called for my follow up comments of "has it gotten to this? You so much ignored both my entrance into the house and now my request for something to eat?" Unfortunately, my last comment surprisingly triggered a snap of "Chyke. Let me advise you to please, get yourself in the kitchen to prepare yourself a meal if you're hungry and must eat. I don't have that time for you now. Yea, you think you're in a restaurant. Amanda this, Amanda that. Am not your house girl, okay? This is America". From my wife, Amanda ;(Chyke slightly pointed to Amanda's direction again).

Chyke continues; you know we were going back and forth against each other with comments and counter comments.

Judge Jones – Yeah, ok, up to this point, did you put your hand on your wife?

Chyke – No my lord.

Judge Jones – Good! You may continue.

Chyke – And right after my next comment of "What did I just hear? "This is America, huh?" – I can now read the handwriting on the wall. Am beginning to think you're getting out of senseless control, and I live to see where this leads to". My wife, Amanda, snapped again and jumped me while repeating the question "Who is getting out of senseless control?" All I was doing was restraining her. But she will not stop as she kicks with her two hands. (Chyke tries to demonstrate Amanda's actions). I let her hands go when I noticed she could no longer kick as she ran out of gas. Then, she ran to the phone and dialed 911. The police will not even listen to my side of the ordeal.

Judge Jones – What do you mean by police will not listen to your side of the ordeal?

Chyke – Yes, my lord. The police officer did not allow me to finish a sentence when he ordered me to leave the house so that he can talk to my wife to calm down the situation as he claimed.

Judge Jones – This supposedly would have been a simple and direct case. But it turns out to look this way; anyway, let's take a 5-minute recess.

Judge Jones – In continuation of ex-parte case between Mrs. Amanda Eze, plaintiff, vs. Mr. Chyke Eze, defendant. May you two take your stands again, please?

Chyke and Amanda get to their respective dock-stands.

Judge Jones - If the defendant's statements are anything to go by, in the area where he quoted the plaintiff of saying, "Chyke, I advise you to get yourself in the kitchen to prepare yourself a meal if you're hungry and must eat. I don't have that time for you now. Yea, you think you're in a restaurant. Am not your house girl, okay? This is America"

I wish to state that in as much as am a proponent of everyone chipping in to help for the smooth running/upkeep of the house/ family. I strongly believe that respect and courtesy to each other cannot be undermined. Especially, to cover up for a shortcoming of not having food for such a man jumping from workplace to classroom when he needs it most despite your being in the house early. Am thinking aloud here, what does the phrase "This is America" mean? I hope this does not have the perception of "This is America", respecter of no person? "This is America", land of disorderliness? "This is America"? Without family values and support? This noble country, "America" deserves better than that, please.

May I state to the plaintiff and if possible, to any other interested party in this courtroom that this is not a divorce court. If for any reasons you choose to take your marriage to this contentious level, you are then advocating for divorce, and I must say you found yourself in the wrong court. If you are keenly interested in divorce, you need go over to the Circuit Court to request for divorce procedure or retain an attorney to help you in that regard.

Judge Jones continues: This case is a total waste of taxpayers' resources. Haven said that I wish to order that the ex-parte order on defendant, Mr. Chyke Eze is hereby revoked.

Chapter Five

The Grover Barber Shop talks between Chyke and his friend, Koffi

Koffi is Chyke's friend. They both met taking classes together when Koffi invited Chyke for hair cut at his barbershop. Here at the barbershop, Koffi works with a colleague by name Jason.

Koffi – Hey Pally! Just the Man I wanted to see. What's going on? Please allow me a few; you are next.

Chyke – Take your time, I am not in a rush.

Chyke takes a seat to peruse at one of the Magazines he picked from the shop's magazine shelve. But it didn't take long for Kofi to beckon him to the barber seat for his haircut.

Koffi - Boy. What is it that I heard? Will this lady ever give you a break to focus on your studies? You know, there is enough stress in this country already not to talk of any ones' stress starting from the house and ending in the house daily. Sincerely speaking, I am not trying to start any sh.t, excuse my French.

Chyke — Believe me, I know what your French means. Trust me, it will soon be over. Guess what? It's hard to believe she would not give up after what she got from the Judge at the court in that last ex-parte order hearing; she still had the guts to call the cops on me again seven days thereafter. It was then that I realized I might end up burning myself trying to figure out this woman. It's a case of total selfishness overshadowed with ego, pride, and arrogance. This is hope utterly lacking.

Koffi — Hey! Make sure you don't rush to judgment. Take your time to evaluate your options; you're a smart guy with good judgments to the best of my knowledge, Ok? But she may have to realize that when one rises too fast, they crash too hard. Because we can guess what this is all about.

Chyke – Thanks, anyway. I will rather be by myself, than with an enemy. I can certainly convince myself that I did my best, they say, "Those who play by the rule, pay what they owe".

As Chyke leaves out of the barbershop, getting into his car to drive off Barber shop parking lot, and Koffi returns inside the barber shop for business as usual

Koffi – God, please help us; Marriage breakages, especially among African couples is becoming an epidemic in this country. In addition, on getting inside, Koffi was surprisingly received by Jason's comments, thus:

Jason – Welcome to my world. Yea! I heard our sisters from Motherland are now becoming too Americanized than the sisters here. Why that?

Koffi – Tell me about it, brother. Didn't you hear me lamenting to God on that? The situation really requires some special prayers with seven different colors of candles.

Jason – Laughing, damn! What did you say? We in this part of the world use to hear Mother land sisters are the best to be with; what is it that is going on now?

Koffi – Yea! It is what it is; African marriages in this crazy place are now becoming nightmares. You get them in and turn around, they are something else, he continues …

Graduation Cook out of one of Mr. & Mrs. Eze's Friends, Mrs. Angie West. Angie West is a devout Christian who chose to cook out as against conventional dancing party for her graduation gets together. This Cook out took place at the back yard of the West's family house.

As visitors tickle into the West's residence from time to time, which include but not limited to,

Chyke Eze came in by himself; Kofi, with his wife, Gloria; Betsy, Anita, and Keisha, came together; Mr. & Mrs. Greg Obasi; and others –

Betsy – Introduces her two friends; Anita and Keisha to Mr. & Mrs. West; Mr. Chyke; Mr. & Mrs. Koffi Bendu, respectively before settling for their seats.

Ed West – Briefly welcomes everyone and introduces Mr. Mike Obasi to lead for opening prayer.

Mike Obasi – Led the gathering in a short, but spiritually captivated prayer focusing more on the celebrant, Angie West, and her family. Lastly, asking for God's journey mercies to all in their travels back to their various homes.

General Socialization, eating, and drinking by all continues at the Cookout for a while, followed by Mr. Ed West's speech:

Ed West – As you eat and drink, please lend me your ears; Ladies, and gentlemen, I wish to use this opportunity to welcome you all ones more making out time out of your crowded schedules to honor this little, but mighty occasion of ours to commemorate the graduation of my one and only, Angie. Just as her name sounds, Angie is a God sent Angel to me and the entire West family. Followed by some rounds of applause from the guests, and repeated yelling of Angie, Angie, Angie continued for a while, …Angie is such an outstanding ambassador of a well natured African woman; I am so glad she attained this milestone, at least as a reward to her hard work, truthfulness and dedication to this family, friends, and well-wishers. Kudos to you Angie, my Sweetheart for a job well done. And lastly, I wish to vehemently express appreciation to everyone present for being part of this outing on behalf of my wife, Angie, and the entire West family. Thanks again for coming and May God Almighty grant you all your individual heart desires as He pleases.

Amanda continues her quest to independence as she and her Real Estate Agent, Anita were spotted visiting couple of town home houses in her bid to buying own house as soon as possible as her planned looming divorce is up and coming.

Chyke and Amanda despise each other with hate and bigotry in their continuous altercations as Amanda moves on with her secret plan of securing a place of residence without Chyke's knowledge and consent.

Amanda – Gets up with a mean looking face and walks into the Kitchen with some mean-spirited song as she dishes out some food, she takes to the dining table to eat, while Chyke seats down in the living room flipping almost through all the TV channels with the remote, looking very disturbed.

Chyke – Takes his turn to go into the kitchen for some food after Amanda was done eating. She walks pass him without a word.

Betsy was spotted stranded on highway and trying to solicit for help as her car stalls:

Betsy – On her cell phone to Amanda – Please Amanda, is your husband, Chyke at home? Am stranded here on the highway with this raggedy car, and I need a tow truck. Do you know if he can be of help?

Amanda - Sorry to hear about your predicament. Hold on, but he is your husband, not mine (whispered by Amanda) as she takes the phone set to Chyke.

Betsy – Good afternoon Chyke, this is Betty. I am stranded here on the highway 195 with a stalled car and I wish to check if you can provide me with information on any reliable tow truck person that I can call to have my car towed.

Chyke – Don't you have "AAA"?

Betsy – No, I don't. I have been procrastinating on that and now Am caught up with this mess. Is there any way you can be of help, please?

Chyke – Okay, I will get back to you as soon as I get something set up for you.

Betsy – Thanks a bunch.

Chapter Six

Amanda and two Male Dayworkers helping her move into her new moderately priced town-home spotted.

Betsy pays Amanda and her daughter, Cindy a visit to their new house. Cindy is a 5-year-old daughter of Amanda and Chyke whose custody was shared both during their divorce saga.

Amanda and Betsy Chatting in the kitchen area of the new house:

Amanda – Please excuse my unfurnished living room.

Betsy – Hey Amanda, I am not new to the system, okay? Am only here to confirm your move in was successful. Am sorry I couldn't be of help due to my work schedule.

Amanda – Don't even let that bother you. You're a friend; indeed, thanks for looking out for us.

Betsy - You're welcome. What are friends for? I must have to let you know that this is the time you need such support, because the path you have chosen is such a path that requires support, no matter how little.

Amanda – Yes, that's what they said. But I hope it will be different once my parents are able to get in here. I am my parents' babe; they mean a lot to me; and we take care of each other.

Betsy – I hope so too. I wish your dream comes true.

Cindy – Runs down from upstairs: Hi Ms. Betsy.

Betsy – Hi Cindy; how're you?

Cindy – Am Good.

Betsy – I hope you like the new house?

Cindy – Yes Miss Betsy, I like it.

Betsy – That's good. Take care of mommy, okay?

Betsy – Amanda, you must know that the most difficult part of moving in is done. The furnishing will come later, and in bits too.

Amanda – That's very true. God is alive; He will provide for us, all.

Betsy – Amen. But I beg to take my leave; I hope you don't mind my brief visit?

Amanda – Not at all, thanks for stopping bye. (Now speaking in low tone as they walk towards the exit door) Just like I previously said,

I seriously look forward to my parents coming in to help reduce Cindy's boredom amongst others.

Betsy – Yea, that will be a major part of it, as she exits the door.

Chyke enters a grocery store for some food items where Keisha was already shopping for groceries; and both accidently met in one of the aisles:

Chyke: Hi Keisha, Betsy's friend, right?

Aisha: Hi, good afternoon. Yea! We met at the graduation party.

Chyke: So, how is your friend, Betsy?

Keisha: She is okay, I believe. I haven't seen her in a while. How is your family? I had you moved to a new house around the corner. I trust it's a good neighborhood.

Chyke: Not exactly.

Keisha: What do you mean, not exactly?

Chyke: eem! I did not move. She moved with our daughter.

Keisha: What's up with that? Do you mean to say you're no more together?

Chyke: Yep.

Keisha: You men! Anyway!

Chyke – Yeah! I see it is always the man's fault. Not so my dear!

Keisha – Really? You must be kidding, that's novel to me, though. Sorry, I don't mean to cut you off; Am kind of in a rush, just stopped by to get some few groceries, but would like to talk more about that later. If you don't mind giving me your phone number, I can give you a call on this sad news. Am sorry to hear that; I thought both of you perfectly complemented each other.

Chyke – Perfection is a relative term my dear, nothing is new in this crazy world of ours anymore. You just get to learn to deal with them as they come.

Keisha – Hey! You get to learn to deal with it if it is true, then.

Chyke – Sure, I have already moved on. Life goes on is the principle.

They both exchanged their contact phone numbers.

Amanda is on a date with this guy, Hector, who happened to talk her to a relationship after several meetings and crossing paths with each other as they worship at the same church.

Amanda had carried out her homework investigation on Hector who she found to be a new immigrant from Nigeria, supposedly.

Amanda and Her friend, Betsy on phone conversation gossip from their different residential locations about Hector, Amanda's newfound love after her outing date with him:

Amanda – Betsy my dear, I was only trying to feel this guy out before making claim of him. And most importantly, you know how it is; "hard to get" is kind of a true thing for a woman from "Mother Land".

Betsy – Yes! But is it true that we African Women indulge in that, "Hard to get" or whatever you call it?

Amanda – Yes. That's our identity. I don't see anything wrong with it. Besides, I strongly believe "A woman's prestige is her heritage."

Betsy – Okay if you say so. However, go ahead to tell me about this guy, Hector.

Amanda – Anyway, he is a Nigerian. He just got here couple of months ago. You know immigrant, now? But he is very thoughtful as he already started taking classes while looking forward to normalizing his status.

Betsy – He must be smart, or he has a good coach.

Amanda – That's what I said too. Meanwhile, although we've being talking over the phone and occasionally seating together in the church, the movie outing was our first date. I am kind of beginning to be excited about him because he seems to be such a gentleman, and he is good looking, with such a unique name, Hector.

Betsy – Am happy for you, Amanda; hang in there, so long as it's what you want, okay!

Amanda – I will my sister. Do I have any other option for now?

Amanda receives an unpleasant international phone call from Nigeria:

While Amanda was in the kitchen preparing breakfast and school lunch, her daughter's take-to-school lunch, the house phone rings grin, grin, and grin. Stops for a while and rings again: grin, grin, and grin. Grin, grin, and grin. Amanda picks up, and yells: Hello, hello, then, listens as the voice on the other side talks.

Amanda – Papa! Papa! Are you kidding me? What was their reason? And did they ask you to come back next time? I mean like, go get some more documents or whatever? She pauses for a while. "God, what then is their problem?

She listens, and after a while, says, I will call you back later today. Hangs up the phone and murmurs to herself, "but I will fight this to the best of my abilities". Immediately, Cindy her daughter comes asking: Mom, what was that? Are you okay?

Amanda – Yes, Am okay. Just get yourself ready before your school bus comes. And, in a low tone, she murmurs again "This is not happening. I hope this is just a dream".

Keisha places a courtesy call to Chyke:

Chyke – As Chyke picks up his call with a musical ring tone, hello!

Keisha – Hello! Hi. This is Keisha.

Chyke – Hi Keisha, how you been? What a big coincidence? I was thinking of calling you some moment ago; but got caught up with some issue that needed my immediate attention.

Keisha – That's okay. Yea! Am calling to let you know that I am not ignoring you, only that it's been so crazy with my workload as this is my company's end of financial year. So, I have been so busy at work, and I even get off work late most times only to get home to be fagged out. I hope to make out time soon. But, meanwhile, this number I called from is my home number; you can call me by it too.

Chyke – Oh! That is nice of you, take your time, now that I know how busy you are, I can call to check on you, ok?

Keisha – That will be nice; I look forward to it

Chyke - But please don't work too hard for we need you! You know what they say, you only work smart, and not too hard?

Keisha – Yes, I do; will do my best to survive it. Thanks, though!

Chyke – You're welcome!

Keisha – Talk to you soon, then.

Chyke – Talk to you, later, cheers!

Amanda pays Betsy a friendly visit:

Betsy – Amanda, what was that your call about? Is Cindy, okay?

Amanda – Yes. Cindy is ok. If She happens not to be ok, I will call 911, she responds to Betsy as she dumps her whole body to Betty's love seat, looking like showers of tears were about to come down her eyes.

Betsy – What then is the matter with you?

Amanda – Takes some time to reluctantly respond; they denied my parents. The crazy U.S. Embassy denied them visa. What Am I to do now? All these craziness around me is for them. They are for them to come and here with me. How can

I be in that house with just Cindy? How will this so-called embassy realize the amount of damage this will be inflicted on me? I am finished. I am not me without them here.

Betsy – Sorry to hear that. But there may be other options like appealing to the case. I wish to ask you to come down and not feel that they're not being here with you as planed as the end of the world in anyway. Rather, should be seen as one of those individual dreams that are hard to come by, not because of your making, may be by God's wish. So, my dear, be strong, pick yourself up to look for alternate way.

Amanda – I hope this is not happening. Not only that it will be damaging to me, but it may also be more damaging to my daughter because I have been hoping on using their presence here to make up for her father's absence.

Betsy – Really!

Chapter Seven

Hector consoles Amanda in her living room. This happens to be the first time Hector comes visiting to Amanda's house. After he was warmly welcomed, and they were seating in the leaving room sipping some soft drinks:

Hector – Amanda, you get to find a way to get over this. I mean, within the confines of reality, your moodiness will not turn things around for any good. But applying plan "B" may yield a better result. Hence, I strongly recommend you stick to your friend's advice of appealing to the case".

Amanda then comported herself as much as she could to the pleasure of her newfound love, Hector as they engage in some other discussions pertaining to church affairs and other little matters of interest to both. Spending ample time together till Hector announces, thus; Dear I beg to take my leave and I hope my presence and the little time we spent helped to cheer you up a bite?

Amanda – Raises her head up a bit and says "Yes, indeed Thanks; I appreciate your stopping by". If your presence doesn't make a difference, whose will?

Hector – In my continuous effort to disabusing your mind and though on that issue, why don't we have launch on your chosen date, time, and venue?

Amanda – Wow darling! That's very nice of you. You're so sweet. Let me check my schedule and then get back to you with a date within the week. Will that work?

Hector – Sure, with all pleasure! I get to run my cab is here.

Amanda – Then be safe. Thanks again.

Hector – You bet, cheers!

As Amanda and Hector arrive for launch at a restaurant, it seems to be a date to cheer Amanda up as she recoups from parents' visa denial. However, at the back of Amada's mind, she intends using the opportunity to intimate herself with Hector who has been such a gentleman, according to her. She is now beginning to feel this to be the relationship she might as well take advantage of for a second chance; as their lovely conversation ensues, thus.

Amanda – So, did you say you are not married?

Hector – Yeah! But, may be looking, I believe am not getting younger at all.

Amanda – But not only that you look matured enough; you also have that good personality that will often attract women to you. So, hearing a person of this your personality still unmarried will be hard to comprehend, not that Am in doubt, anyway.

Hector – That may be true, I have gotten close to being married couple of years ago, but she left me for another man. And because I had seen her to be the love of my life, it's been hard for me to forgo the disappointment. However, you know time heals every wound, and is about getting over it.

Amanda – Sorry to hear that. You know we all have our bitter stories to tell; I've had my share of ugly relationships, too.

Hector – But I am getting to know it's part of growing up.

Amanda – Yes, indeed. Anyway, what do you intend to achieve with me? You know I am a divorcee with a child?

Hector – That's' not a problem to me at all, "I only hope it works out well for us", he said, romantically holding her hand, and caressing it with tenderness.

Amanda's visit to Hector's residence – Beginning from Hector ushering her into his little palace, as he calls it. This visit was meant to elevate their relationship to its deserved amorous level to show case her full and committed interest with Hector as Amanda thinks.

Hector – Welcome to my little Palace. I hope you don't mind the smallness.

Amanda – No, not at all. You must start from somewhere, just like everyone else. Tell you what? It's small, but classy and sexy; I truly, truly, like it.

Hector – Thanks, you made my day. What do I fix you? I have wine, Orange Juice…

Amanda – You omitted water.

Hector – I hope you're not asking for just water?

Amanda – Laughs! What if I do? Just kidding. Let me have some wine if it's red wine.

Hector – Sure, it is a good one too. He dashes out to his kitchen and comes out with bottle of red muscado; he reaches for the bottle and pups it open to pour to the two wine glasses in his hand and passes one to Amanda for a little toss before they start drinking.

Amanda – How did you find this unique place?

Hector – Oh! You seem to really like it?

Amanda – Yes; did you think it was a tease when I said I truly like it?

Hector – Moves closer to her, beaming with smiles. And after a couple of minutes.

Amanda – This wine seems to be getting on me so quick.

Hector – I hope not that quick because I ordered some food if you don't mind? That was to the extent their conversation got to open till both woke up to find themselves in nude in Hector's queen-sized bed with sparkling white beddings with some decorative designs at the edge craving for the food previously mentioned of.

Hector and Amanda continued in their good relationship to the admiration of close friends and well-wishers after it was consolidated with her constant visits and some sleep overs to Hector's residence as they were seen as inseparables all over the town. Amanda could' ask for any better.

While on the other hand, Chyke was having a blast with Keisha in their own way as he shows up with her to a Sports Bar their agreed venue to watch 2016 Super Bowl championship game (Super Bowl 50). This year's Super Bowl taking place in Santa Clara, California between Carolina Panthers led by Cam Newton representing the NFC and Denver Broncos led by Peyton Manning representing the AFC of the National Football League (NFL) on this 7th day of February 2016. The NFL is made up of 32nd franchise teams. Also, in attendance at this game show are, his friend, Koffi, Jason and some other employees and friends from the barbershop, together with couple of Chyke's colleagues at work. Chyke and Keisha take their seats as Keisha and Koffi's barbershop guys briefly introduced themselves to each other, as they happen to meet for the first time.

Koffi – Boy, I thought you weren't coming because of your work?

Chyke – Not Super bowl game, pally; I was able to make a swift switch.

Koffi – True, not for this all-American game.

Chyke – You know Koffi, one gets to make himself available for this yearly ritual after all the hard work and stress in this country; you get to utilize opportunities of this sort to ease out stress. And, as my girl doesn't work weekends, we felt it's a golden opportunity hanging out with friends.

Koffi – Tell me about it. That was why I couldn't comprehend your excuse of not coming when I first spoke to you on the phone last week. Am glad you made it, anyway. And Keisha thanks for coming out to be with us.

Keisha – My pleasure. Thanks!

Chyke calls the waitress to order some drinks and food for his girl, Keisha, and himself.

As Keisha excuses herself to use the rest room prior to the arrival of their food, Chyke and Koffi engaged in some "boys' talk" pertaining her, thus:

Koffi – How is your relationship with her coming along?

Chyke – Good! So far so good, I am having a blast.

Koffi – So, do you think she may be the one?

Chyke – I don't intend jumping into early judgment or try making any policy statement so soon. I can only say "The old is past and gone, and the new is taking possession of the ticking time". When one tries to make it with someone from same cultural and geographical hemisphere without success, then you're forced to look outside the box so to say. But hey, don't get me wrong, we are taking it one day at a time, per my last experience, and she very much understands that. Besides, the maturity she exhibits as you pointed out some time ago carries its' own sour and hard to swallow taste that I believe might help us comfort each other and edify one another as she disclosed.

Koffi – Don't blame you at all; no one expect you to rush any damn thing; for "once beaten, twice share" is a saying of the good old days!

Keisha – Comes out from the rest room; did I miss anything?

Chyke – Not at all, sweetie; Just senseless "boys' talk"

Keisha – It doesn't surprise me.

Koffi – Yes indeed, Keisha gal!

Super Bowl 50th game played February 5th, 2017, at NRG Stadium, Houston, Texas between Atlanta Falcons representing NFC and New England Patriots representing AFC with the half time entertainment show performed by lady Gaga ended in overtime 34/28 in favor of Patriots of New England. Hence, making Patriots world champions for the season with Tom Brady winning his fifth Super Bowl Championship (Ring) with New England under Coach Bill Belichick.

Chapter Eight

Chyke and Keisha were on their routine romantic bedtime phone conversation when Keisha reminded him of her upcoming birthday in about two weeks' time and Chyke surprised her with promise of a birthday treat. She is to be accompanied by any two of her choice friends to her favorite restaurant, Outback Steakhouse Restaurant on Saturday presiding her birthday date that falls on Thursday. Chyke and Keisha had established likeness for Outback Steakhouse Restaurant, especially with their hot coffee bread appetizer and grilled chicken salad with ranch dressing for Chyke and fried shrimps and house salad with Caesar dressing amongst others for Keisha.

Keisha – This is a good surprise babe; I was not expecting such. I thought both of us would just have gone out on our own for a quiet time.

Chyke – It's okay, after all this is your 1st one since our coming together, and I feel your friends should have a feel of it as well, and most importantly, so they could help declare war against any other interested party on my behalf.

Keisha – Really? You are f... king nuts, boy! So, you're that territorial?

Chyke – Maybe **if** you say so! Just kidding sweetie.

Keisha – I don't even mind, is okay by me. It's good to show that commitment, after all.

Chyke – Cool then, thanks for your better understanding.

Keisha – You're welcome. But want you to know am in it for good, I've already taken myself out of any guys' reach. Am a one-man girl all the way.

Chyke – You made my day, gal! I appreciate that, and I promise you my best all the way as you said, too.

Keisha – Wow! That's so sweet, what a lovely night!

Chyke – My pleasure, dear!

Keisha – Trust you don't mind, you've talked me to sleep with these good promises of yours, and I would want to wake with carryover of them to start my tomorrow.

Chyke – That will be nice, then. I trust you'll dream of me.

Keisha – Are you kidding me? That's exactly what am talking about. It's not real if I don't.

Chyke – Okay then, night, night!

Keisha – You too, thanks!

Chyke, Keisha, and her friends spotted at Outback Steakhouse Restaurant at Laurel industrial Park near Best Western Hotel; Chyke surprisingly showed up with his buddy, Koffi and his wife for Keisha's birthday eat out:

In the middle of their birthday dinner meal, a group of Outback Steakhouse servers showed up with a decorated birthday cake and some lighted candles, singing happy birthday song in honor of the birthday girl, Keisha in in conjunction with others on their dining table. And right after the last stance of the song, Chyke called to everyone's attention, with; please give me a minute as he stood up.

Chyke - Keisha, are you enjoying your day?

Keisha - Yes indeed, babe!

Chyke – Pulls a tiny tine box from his pocket to grab the content of a ring as he shoves the dining table creating some space for himself as he goes on one of his knees to say, "Keisha, you came into my life to turn negativities around for good. You make me feel complete at a time I would have been in pains. So, I wish to keep the goodness I've found in you forever. Please I wish to ask, would you marry me?"

Meanwhile, Keisha could be heard in low tone saying, this's not happening, this's not happening as she buries her face in her two palms.

Chyke – Now, frantic, and nervous, asked again; would you marry me?

Keisha – Yes of course, you're a gift; you don't reject a gift, you appreciate it. I will marry you for sure my birthday gift. And I'll forever treasure you.

Here comes a female voice, presumably from one of Keisha's friends, wow! That's sweet; you go gal!! As Chyke went on with his nervousness to slide the ring to Keisha's finger and grabbed her just as she jumped to his embrace for some protracted warm kisses followed by all round greetings of congratulations as the restaurant staffers dispersed. Keisha's engagement ring is a moderately priced 10kt diamond ring Chyke acquired from Kay Jewelers.

And as they settled:

Koffi – Gently whispered into Chyke's ears; boy, you're full of surprises. You caught me off guard on this.

Chyke – Yeah pally, we'll talk about it, for sure.

As others left to their various destinations at the end of this outing, Keisha requested Chyke to accompany her to her residence to drop off her car so they both can ride to his residential place in Burtonsville, Maryland together. And so was it as they both spent the weekend together as newly engaged.

On this day, Chyke and Koffi were on casual telephone conversation; Koffi reiterated Keisha's birthday/ engagement outing, thus.

Koffi – Yeah Chyke, I wish to bring up our suspended surprise you handed over to everyone on that day as part of the dinner?

Chyke – Yes Koffi, I thought of not waiting any longer, and decided to make it happen. She's a very appreciative and non-repulsive girl. What you witnessed and heard in her response to my proposal in the restaurant, that's just what she is for real. She's so appreciative of any gestures that come her way. She's pure and genuine. I've never felt so good about a person. Trust me after a taste of sour; you will be delighted once a candy is shoved into your God given mouth. I wasn't either expecting perfection on the other hand, and so, this's it. In all comparisons to what I had prior, I regard her statue of life liberty and I pray she retains that; trusting we'll be there for each other in every twist and turns.

Koffi – You know, I've never questioned your decisions, and I wish you the very best.

Chyke – Thanks a lot.

As about a month was past gone that Chyke handed his unexpected marriage proposal to Keisha, they both spend time together in either of their apartments. On this day, both were spending the weekend over at Keisha's place of residence when Keisha engaged Chyke in a sudden conversation to Chyke's amazement, thus:

Keisha – Hey Chyke, this place has been awfully quiet for some time now, and I have been holding back on back on this and now not anymore.

Chyke – What? What happened? What did I do wrong, Keisha? I thought it's been nice and lovely for us?

Keisha – Not at all, dear. Sorry if I sounded dramatic, it was mere anxiety.

Chyke – So, what's this about?

Keisha – Hang on please; let me get you a cup of drink for putting in that mood to cool off.

Chyke – But your suspense is messing me up the more, please. Just spill it

But Keisha would not stop at that as she headed to the dining area and re-emerged with a half full glass of their last night left over red wine.

Keisha – Here it is, love of my life.

Chyke – And?

Keisha – I hope you don't mind my bothering you, please?

Chyke – Go ahead, am listening!

Keisha – With complete gladness, I wish to say you handed me the most pleasant surprise of my life with your shocker proposal. Though, it's been more than a month now, am yet to get over it with happiness and delight. And it's on that note I wish to say that with the help of my best friend you know too well that can put together a little get well for both of us to the Island of Aruba. I please beg of you not to say no to it.

Chyke – Is this this your craziness is all about? Keisha, please don't rush to this for we have a lot of planning together to take us to such level when time is right.

Keisha – I very much get you, but this's my little get to believe it outing from me to you. It's only a three-night, three day all you can eat package. Drinks only on us, and both of us are light drinkers, making it very affordable. Please, don't reject it for the sake of my friend who took time to get this deal for me. We'll leave here on

Friday after work to come back on Monday, hence, would only loose Monday workday from work. Aruba, I heard is a very lovely Island and I being longing to be there with the right group till you showed up with this loving personality of yours, so I felt the time is right. May I also say that the bill is on me? But you may pick the drink bills if you choose to help.

Chyke – So, why not then reserve it for future use for …

Keisha – Oh! You already have that in mind? But there're so many other good places we can explore together. But, like I said, this is just to honor your proposal.

Chyke – I didn't say pass whatever you have in mind, though!

Keisha – I get it, my birthday gift. We must get there and beyond, IJN.

Chyke – Heard you but allow me time to ponder over it.

Keisha – Please darling, I need to close this deal unless I lose it. Please say yes at least for my friend's sake so as not to make her efforts fruitless. Please dear!

Chyke – Okay, cool. But I need details of it later.

Keisha – This's why I feel blessed since you came into my life. Bless your heart, sweetheart! Aruba, here we come. My one and only, I'll forever remain grateful and loyal to you, I pledge. Thank you! Thank you! Thank you!

Chyke – You're welcome! You're welcome! Am glad I got my sanity back after all that your dramatic suspense.

Keisha – Sorry dear, I'll make it up to you.

And after about 20 months into Amanda and Hector's love relationship, Amanda was concerned when in about three days Hector was missing in action (MIA) as he surprisingly never reached out to her and couldn't be reached either on his phone. So, on this blissful day, she decides to make a quick check to Hector's residence at College Park also called the "University City" housing the elite University of Maryland (Fear the Turtle).

As she pulls her car by the roadside in front of the building and goes to knock on the door –

Landlord – Answers the door from inside and in few minutes opens the door. May I help you?

Amanda – Yes please, my name is Amanda; am here for Hector, is he in?

Landlord – Hector? Hector is out of the country; he left about three days ago.

Amanda – Do you know when he's coming back?

Landlord – I didn't say he travelled. I said he left the country. He's gone back to his country. He's done with the academic training he was here for; I believe he called it a postgraduate in-service study that ended about last three weeks. Hector works for the Federal Government of Nigeria, according to him, although he talked less about it.

Amanda – How come he didn't let me know?

Landlord – I hope he is not indebted to you in anyway? I know he's not that kind of a person.

Amanda – He's not what? Yes indeed, he covered his dirty tracks well like a pro; men are devil incarnate, she murmurs.

Landlord – What was that?

Amanda – Never mind. The estranged wife of Chyke still in disbelieve, said, "I hope this's not really happening, otherwise, I am dead as disco.

Landlord – I was even cleaning his unit for prospective renters before I heard your knock on the door. Although, he is such a private person, I can say he may not have planned it the way it turned out because he had planned of his wife joining him for the duration of her vacation so they could shop together before leaving. But incidentally, their little baby got very sick, so he had to leave to see them right away as he said. You're welcome to come in to see for yourself.

Amanda – No, it doesn't call for that. I believe you, and believe what men can do, "turns around and headed back to her car".

Landlord – Politely yells, nice meeting you young lady.

Amanda –While seating in her car with head lowered to the steering, ranting in lamentation, "Lord, what have I done wrong? Why is my world crumbling on me? "I hope this is not real, I pray. God! How and who can I share the story of my life with?

PART 2

"Africa, Our Mother-Land"

"Mama Africa"

Pondering on it, I graciously invite you to brainstorm with me on what seem to be wrong with us all from the Motherland, Africa. Not just in the context of this bookwork, rather in broader scheme of life. Africans or Blacks, descendants of Continent of Africa are commonly referred to as Africans, African Americans, Negros, Nero, Noah, Mahogany, Nubian, Ebony, and Blacks. But why have we as a people, politically, economically, and sociologically disenfranchised ourselves in the scope of life due to maladministration, lack of patriotism greed, selfishness, and disunity amongst others despite all God given abundant natural resources within our beck and call? I strongly believe this milestone question may begin to be addressed from the following:

Our so-called leaders uncontrollably loot money from us to send to the colonial masters through:

Money Laundry

Accounts in Swiss Banks

Accounts in Europe, and United States

Sending their Children to Colonial Masters' Schools overseas

Buying Houses abroad

Non-ceasing abroad vacations

Constant overseas' trips for medical treatments and check-ups

Unreasonable Materialistic Tendencies

Autocratic/Authoritarian government Systems

It never crosses their minds and thought to invest back the stolen money into their society for development/posterity, to the least.

Then, at the lower echelon, an average black person wants the best things of life at the expense of investments, such as:

Expensive Cars

Brand Name Apparels/Shoes

Brand name handbags

Extended Family System

Exorbitant Funeral Rights

Jealousy/Envy

Flamboyancy

In all, Africans in general and Nigerians are so uncontrollably into items of swanky qualities.

Here in the United States of America for instance, about 93% of blacks killed are victims of same race for no apparent course; blacks kill their fellow blacks daily instead of wanting to see them succeed, despite the following prominent inventions by blacks, as recorded:

Alexander Mills invented the Elevator,

Richard Spikes invented the Automatic Gearshift, Joseph Gambol invented the Super Charger System for internal Combustion Engine,

Garrett A. Morgan invented the Traffic Lights,

John Standard invented the Refrigerator,

Albert R. Robinson invented the Electric Trolley,

Lee Barrage invented the Typewriter Machine,

Charles Brooks invented the Street Sweeper, and others.

Pertinent to say these plights are mainly accomplished in developed countries like the United States of America with facilities and infrastructures set up to attain such feat while they are totally lacking in almost all African countries/continent. Even with the 1st and oldest world university recorded to be founded and established in Africa, the University of Al-Karaouine in Morocco in the year 859AD by Fatima Al-Fihri without any recorded pivotal discoveries or inventions to its' credit. Besides, the institution is not even ranked amongst elite universities of the world. The next two Universities following the establishment of the University of Al-Karaouine are, the Universities of Bologna, Italy, founded in 1088 as the oldest in Europe and Oxford University, presumed to be founded in 1096.

In my Candid perception, it is so obvious that the only part of economics blacks comprehend is consumption; we do not understand the importance of building wealth; we must understand that the fundamental rule of world economics is wealth creation and keeping such within your racial group. Every successful African wants to spend his money in the country of his colonial masters, hence continually enriching the colonial masters at the detriment of his Motherland. Statistics shows that only about 6% of black money goes back into black communities. We must realize that not preserving wealth is only but our fault. Blacks must take responsibilities. Black lives matter more when blacks unite.

Embezzlement and misappropriation of funds is so synonymous with African leaders from their highest levels of political positions to the lowest levels of community and town unions. Situations where association presidents were involved in check misappropriations and other irregularities without proper accountability and practice of simple separation of duties is a common practice within and amongst Africans/African leaders. In addition, when such selfish, irresponsible, and absurd practice of financial and administrative recklessness of theirs is talked about, their screwed defense is always blackmailed and victimization. Some even resort to lynching as to silence your candid opinion. (I recently became a victim to such stupendous behavior, which must never be an impediment to my honesty and sincerity as I keep a close watch around me, with pending legal action alternatively, while my family observes with keen interest). That is very overwhelming uncivilized African thing that is so unfortunate in their leadership/administrative arena. Their clench to positions and powers is just to enrich themselves and their families at the expense of the masses who entrusted them with positions they are designated to serve.

We must insidiously fight corrupt leaders who run down our associations', communities', and countries' economies. Most importantly, black leaders must adapt to complete democracy, making room for full disclosures and transparencies in governance as against autocratic and authoritarian tendencies. Also, to mention as a canker worm is our overwhelming ignorant over dependence on colonial masters' system for sustenance due to lack of creativity being destructive to our effective existence and operations. For instance, Nigeria copies and adopts America's three-tier system, also called the Federal system of government but executes total abstract in practice. Even in whole, claims practicing American system of voting democracy, but leaves out the "Electoral Votes" aspect of it designed for voter fraud check and election rigging instead of creating and formulating own system that works for us. Hence, undermining differences in ethnicity, tradition, and culture; Africa, you never can go wrong being yourself, being original, making it your own, and being creative. Africans, we must please break your own new grounds!

Also, our leaders must resort to funding and financing locals of Nnewi Spare-parts and Aba

Shoemakers' initiatives and others of their likes in helping them thrive to acceptable world standards against over dependent on foreign made. Just in retrospect, the debunked Republic of Biafra's Research and Production (RAP) Unit, makers of Cannon (Ogbunigwe or Ojukwu-Bucket), Home-made Armored Cars (Biafran Red Devil), Rockets, Beer from Cassava, Engine Oil from Coconut, Shore Batteries, and Hand Grenade making Engineers and Technicians were dishonorably dismissed and discharged after the Civil war with ignominy. A people (Biafrans) who demonstrated ingenuity in the mist of unspeakable adversities, had their ideas, good work, and creativity suppressed, destroyed, and killed by sheer act of punishment, vendetta, and jealousy by Nigerian autocratic leaders as against retaining them for improvement to better standards. Pertinent to mention that my dad late Bertram M. Agoha was a victim to this act of senseless and cruel behavior. Incidentally, till date Nigerian Military department spends billions in purchase of such military hard wares from colonial masters. In view of the above and other political and economic ill-treatment of Biafra zone as step child, being challenged and threatened by their technological awareness as advised by some of the western world who compared Biafra as African Japan, I stand not to waiver to say, with, within, or without the nation, Nigeria, Biafra must be allowed to exit as a sovereign state or Nigeria now seen as a failed system, be renegotiated on the basis of geographical zones allowing each zone control its resources and destinies aimed at fostering healthy competition to enhance economic growth, development, and progress on the basis of fairness, equity, rancor, egalitarianism, and justice for all. For people of Biafra region will for eternity remember over 45,000 innocent men, women, and children butchered and massacred from around May 1966 to 1970 by Nigerians led by British tanks and Russian planes (Genocide) while the rest of the world watched in silence. "Let my people go" is a biblical saying of the ages. However, in most amicable possible manner without bloodshed as to foster continues friendliness.

The diversity amongst us must be utilized as advantageous as against disadvantageous and destructive menace to our unity and progress.

A presumed world leader (Israeli Leader) recently delivered a scathing critique of

Africans, thus; "Africans cried and fought for independence, yet have failed to rule themselves. They have mineral resources but cannot put them to any meaningful use for their growth and development, letting the colonial masters come pick whatever valuable and leaving out whatever is with them". While British Lord Macaulay in his address to British Parliament on February 2, 1835, proposed thus, "That they replace African old and ancient education and culture to make them think that all that is foreign, and English is good and greater than their own. With that, they will lose their self-esteem and their native culture and will become what we want them, a truly dominated nation. Also, Encyclopedias Britannica has thus, recorded on Negro; "NEGRO, Homo pelli nigra, a name given to a variety of human species who are entirely black. Of the vices, the most notorious of these seem to be the portion of unhappy race: idleness, treachery, revenge, cruelty, impudence, stealing, lying, profanity, nastiness, and intemperance, said to have extinguished the principles of natural law, and to have silenced the reproofs of their conscience. They are strangers to every sentiment of compassion and are an awful example of corruption of man when left to him."

So, are we truly victims or liable and deserving of such scathing impressions of us, Africans? From my perspective, it's absurd that a continent such as ours with the greatest and best natural resources will fail to turn things around with all there is within us to our maximum potentials than letting such be for the continued sustenance of those who exploited, mocked, and enslaved us. Understandably the colonial masters from Britain as recently confessed and disclosed by one of the perpetrators, Mr. Smith on how they sowed seed of confusion and discord to a country like Nigeria for instance to frustrate its' potentials. Yes, given they did what they had to do in the world international political and economic arena for control. Their act was patriotism and selfless service to their home countries compared to your indispicable political vice and corruption that doubles down to diversion of state funds to fighting and settlement of court cases, for crying out loud. Please spare me your wolf cries; it's strongly believed the best performs better when challenged. Wake up to smell the coffee for time is of the essence to turn things around for good without further ado.

It is mind boggling to say that African problems may be obviously summarized as compounded by government maladministration or mismanagement, congressional impasse, and religious misguidedness. While the two formers seem to be embedded in the fabrics of the continent from inception, the latter is a new evil that has crippled in as shocker. Most new religious leaders of this continent, especially Nigeria are far from being preachers meant truthfully to proclaim the word of God. They are more interested in ostentatiousness and even some unclassified immoralities than true words of God for new devoted converts. Churches are no longer where Christians are found on the Lord's Day, rather where you are entertained someway and somehow; where the biggest donors are recognized and given the front roll seats, hence inducing undue and unnecessary rivalry and competitions amongst members. Salvation is far from what most of our religious leaders are preaching and delivering. Most of our new generation churches and their leaders are more into seed sewing, instant and quick miracle manifestations, prosperity, and break through. The old religious saying, "Fortune favors a cheerful giver" has so much been misinterpreted to mislead for personal gains. Spreading of misleading message of instant success is turning our country into a country of laziness and greed to the benefits of preachers and religious leaders who have turned themselves into quick and sudden millionaires and billionaires at the expense of their ignorant and poor followers. God is not a rewarder of laziness and filthy wealth; we all must comprehend. A time of reflection and soul searching is now as to avert destruction for Christianity has played big role to destruction of Nigeria today that is not what is meant or intended to. While it is given that our leaders in government have failed in their primary duties of nation building and provision of simple amenities and infrastructures, our religious leaders can make a difference by leading in community building, cleaning, creativity, and innovation through communal efforts for a start.

I therefore suggest, if not recommend that African in general and Nigerian leaders particularly must wake up to spirit of patriotism and nation building as to stand the taste of time in leadership and development. Have you ever pondered on why in the rankings of 40 most religious countries of the world the top 10 with Ethiopia leading the queue and Nigeria sitting in ninth comfortable position right after Ghana are amongst the poorest and underdeveloped countries of the world? Not to mention also that nine out of these 10 leading nations are African countries. Then, where does that put us despite all our religious zealousness? "Just some food for thought"

Just for investigative academic purposes. Considering different functional religious denominations all over the world, a school of thought recently argued that Africans' abandonment of their ancestral God in pursuit and acceptance of foreign God introduced by colonial masters triggered a nonperformance course put on Africans by our ancestral God calls to be investigated for better clarity and sense of purpose. (You may kill the message and not the messenger depending on your take to this thought). For Instance, it has been established to be factual that, Nigeria as the largest Black Nation in the world and the most populous nation in Africa, Nigerians are setting the pace and becoming the standard by which nationalities measure their progress as Nigerians are one of the most, if not the most educated immigrant community in the U.S. Nigerians outperform their peers from other nations. The designer of Chevrolet Volt, Jelani Aliyu is from Sokoto State, Nigeria. The wealthiest black man and woman on mother earth are Nigerians, Aliko Dangote, and Mrs. Folorunsho Alakija with no trace of any criminal or wrongdoing in their business empire building are Nigerians. South Africa could not have ended apartheid and achieved black rule if not for the leadership role Nigeria played. Before the establishment of streetlights in European cities, ancient Benin Kingdom of Nigeria had streetlights fueled by palm oil. The first television station in Africa was NTA Ibadan (1960), long before Ireland had their RTE station. Unfortunately, Nigeria as a nation has nothing tangible or significant to show in infrastructural and economic development to all the acclaims.

In all, I seem to lean towards the school of thought that states; wealth is generation oriented. We as a people are at the bottom of the economic hierarchy and must not spend more. We must socialize to be united as against being disunited. Progress is a group and team effort; we must converge to get it done with the right infrastructural apparatus in the right places.

Suffice to say, there are yet some overwhelming setbacks like, clan-based mentality, religious fanaticism, lack of adequate navigable seas, and harsh weather conditions embedded in this topic that explicitly need being explored. Hence, all are welcome to engage in continuous discussion on this issue in helping build our nations/continent; tilting not believing there is no discrimination in creation, otherwise a course on our black nation, despite the seed of discord and regression sowed in the continent by the British. If not, we will continuously remain economically colonized and loose our deserving place in history.

"Biafra, God's Chosen"

I was spending a period of half calendar year in Israel within and amongst Nigerian community in general and Igbos when and where this topic of Igbos as descendants of Israel was introduced; Genesis 29:30, Jacob had twelve sons; Ruben, Simon, Levi, Judah, Daniel, Naphtali, Gad, Asher, Issachcher, Zebulun, Joseph, and Benjamin… The seventh son, Gad (Gen. 46:16) had seven sons, namely: Ziphon, Haggi, Shunni, Ezbon, Eri, Arodi, and Areli. Sometime in Middle East, famine struck, and Jacob moved with his family and with about 70 other relations to Egypt. However, before then, Joseph, who was the 11th son of Jacob had been sold to Egypt by is brothers as the bible tells us…, where he was later made Governor General under then King Pharaoh. As time progressed, they suffered persecution from the hands of Egyptians, but Eri, the 5th son of Gad foresaw the long effect of the persecution and wickedness from the Egyptians and he decided to leave with his two younger brothers, Arodi and Areli together with one of his half-brothers, and they travelled through Ethiopia, Sudan and down towards West Africa through River Nile and landed at a place known as Aguleri (Around 1305 BC). Today, this is known as Omabala River in Anambra State. Eri established and lived close to this Omabala River and became wise and wealthy like his great grandfather, Abraham (Abiama in Igbo language). This is said to be why Anambra State claims to have the highest number of richest people in Igbo land for the least. Eri gave birth to five children: Agulu, Atta, Oba, Hebrew/Igbo, and Menri. Agulu as the 1st son stayed back and established in the place known tin the present day as AguluERI (Agulu son of Eri) in Anambra

State. While Atta moved upward north and established in a place called Igala, today known as Igala Kingdom. In the present-day dispensation, the overall King of Igala is known and addressed as "Atta of Igala" in Kogi State. Oba, the third son left and founded a place known as Oba Kingdom, known to be in Anambra State today. Hebrew changed to mean Higbo or Igbo was a very powerful spiritual man and this seem to be why people from this area till date as I gathered are very spiritual. Later, he left and founded Igbo-Ekiti, Igbo-Adagbe, Igbo-Eze (All within Nsukka, Enugu State and Parts of Anambra State, now). Menri left and founded a place known as "AgukwuNri" NRI Kingdom. Arodi also moved to a place known as "Aro-Chukwu"… He was very industrious and good with Arts and Crafts. Arodi later gave birth to Nembe, Ngwa, Abakaliki, Ogoni, Afikpo, Aro-Ikot Ekpene (Today's Akwa Ibom), Aro-Echie (Today's Rivers State), and Arodinzuogu (In today's Imo State). During slave trade, Aro spread all over the world – Evidence of present day's presence of Igbos all the world as the most travelled – Aro Festival is always celebrated in Cuba till date, and in a recent Television interview a well-travelled European sarcastically stated that the only country Igbos are not seen present was Somalia. Areli was a man full of wisdom and this area's native tongue is today's descendants known as "Central Igbo". It is also assumed that this area has the highest number of graduates and professors in Igbo land. Areli gave birth to: Owerre, Umuahia, Diobu, Okigwe, Orlu, Nkwerre, Elele, Mba-Ise, Mba-Ano, etc. Pertinent to mention that Eri's half bother as earlier mentioned moved as well and founded Ijaw and some parts of present-day Edo State and many other parts of Niger Delta (Imagine the similarities today).

For verifications, in Aguleri today, there is a particular house known as OBI GAD (House of Gad). Gad was the 7th son of Jacob (Gen. 29:30) and Gad begets five sons of which the last three (Eri, Arodi, and Areli and their half-brother left Egypt to West Africa). The Obi Gad was a resting and relaxing place for Eri and his brothers, so they named it "Obi Gad" to honor their father, Gad the 7th son of Jacob. Just recently in Igbo land, this Obi/Obu was/is known to be the house/place for elders' resting place, gathering and meetings and this is the reason every Igbo family build or has Obi/Obu in their family compound. Ada means first daughter in Israel (Gen. 4:19-20), same in Igbo land and parts of its' surrounding neighborhoods, like Benue State. Before an Igbo man makes a contribution in public gathering, he shouts "Igbo Kwenu" and his kinsmen respond "" Yah", and "Yah" is short form of "Yahweh", and "Yahweh" is the name of Jewish God – "Jehovah-Yahweh".

Israelis were known to manufacture about 80% of world weapons just like Igbos manufactured 80% of all the weapons used by Biafra during the civil war, which no other African ethnicity has or can. This was the concern to other world leaders when they voiced their opinion against the existence of African-Japan as they called it and hence brainwashed and supported the Nigerian side to carry out genocide against Biafra. It is customary and tradition that Igbos carry home their dead just like Israelis (Gen. 49:29-50). Just like Israelis, Igbos are led and ruled by Elders and Priests. An Israeli Ambassador, Noah Katz once said, Igbos are Jews (Nigerian Daily Sun Newspaper of 28 March 2004)

Just as God (Jehovah-Yahweh) has said, "Israelis are my chosen (Countless verses of the bible). Respectfully, Igbos or Biafrans as descendants of Israel are God's chosen and must not be marginalized for, they are Nigeria's engine block particularly, and Africa's at large. Indisputably, Igbos or Biafrans have the technological, industrial, business, educational and environmental expertise to bring to Africa's table of development. Igbos/Biafrans are the sons of the Most-High God, the God of Abraham (Abiama/Chukwu-Abiama).

FYI – The Igbos occupy the area known as Biafran region, the Southeastern region of present-day Nigeria. Biafran region has become an emerging global tribal region with huge population density of about 1,351 persons per sq. km. and largest concentration of human and material resources in African Continent.

Summary

This book is divided into two major parts: Part one that is subdivided into eight chapters focuses on marriage relationships and disappointments, saying; though with good intent of starting families with persons of similar or same ethnicity and cultural background as an overwhelming global practice sounds plausible and intriguing, this literary work of mine, "Paid In Own Token" reveals otherwise. It goes to say that it is set on premise that marriage disappointments encountered on initial hopes and aspirations based on set prejudice maybe redeemed with openness of mind to better or other alternatives, per awareness. It reveals "Unity In Diversity", while "Evil Begets Evil". While part two of the book investigates some underlying issues of African Continent and Africans or Blacks as a people in relation to underdevelopment and internal wrangling, despite their countless human and natural resources.

Author Biography

U.S. Citizen by naturalization, Nigerian by birth, Anelechi Bon Agoha is also author of the following two books: "Your Destiny Is Your Choice" and "Second-Generation Slavery".

In 2005, Anelechi Bon starred in a U.S. based African home-movie, "Far from Home". He studied Cardiovascular Technology at Sanford Brown Institute, Maryland, Criminal Justice at University of Maryland Global Campus, and Purchasing & Supply Management at the Federal Polytechnic, Owerri, Imo State, Nigeria. Anelechi Bon Agoha is a family-oriented man blessed with three incredible children.